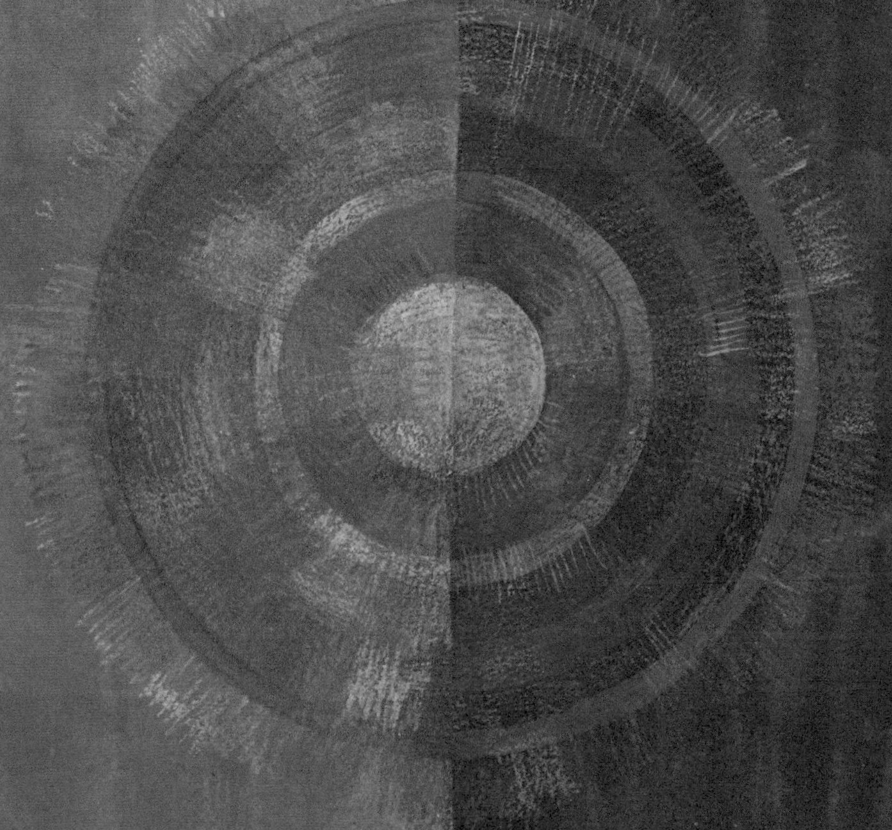

WHY THE SUN WAS LATE

By
BENJAMIN ELKIN

Illustrated by
JEROME SNYDER

Parents' Magazine Press
New York

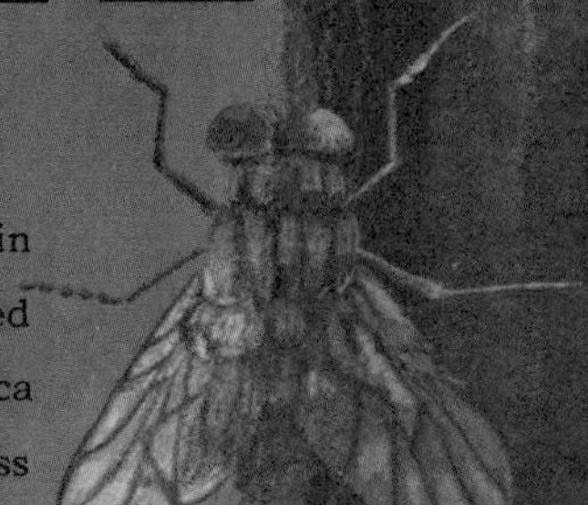

Printed in the United States of America
Library of Congress
Catalog Card Number: AC 66-10094

It was a lazy afternoon. In the jungle
an old, weak tree waited for just one small breeze
to make it fall. But the air was calm
and there was no breeze.

Then along came a buzzing fly. He stopped to rest
on a leaf of the old tree. And that one touch
was enough. The tired tree gave a sigh, and then
toppled over with a crash.

Buzz! said the amazed fly. "Who would have
guessed that I, by myself alone, would be
strong enough to knock down a tree?"
And, puffed up with pride, he flew away
to see what else he could do.

Soon the fly saw two boys climbing another tree
to gather nuts. "Here's where I have some fun,"
thought the fly. "Won't those boys be surprised
when I push them right off the tree!"

The fly buzzed from one boy to the other,
trying to make them fall. But the mighty strength
that had knocked down the tree seemed to be gone.
All the fly could do was tickle them on the nose.

"Oh, go away!" said one of the boys.
He swung wildly at the fly with his hand.
But instead of hitting the fly he hit a branch.
And that blow really started something...

It so happened that three squirrels
had been sitting on that very same branch.
Down fell the three squirrels. And they landed
right on top of four snakes who were
sleeping in the grass.

The four startled snakes jumped up.
They slithered off in the grass without
stopping to look. And they blundered into
a herd of five elephants.

The five elephants trumpeted with fear. They rushed madly across the field. Crash! They bumped headfirst into a hill. The trees on the hill swayed and trembled. And out of one tree fell a nest with six eggs.

Then the poor mother bird began to cry.
"Oh, my darling babies. Their shells are cracked.
Now my heart is broken, too. Never, never, never
shall I sing again."

All that afternoon and all that night,
the mother bird was silent. At last it was
time for dawn, but the bird did not sing
her usual wake-up song. Now everyone knows
it's the song of a bird that wakes the sun.
Without that song, the sun slept on and on.
And the day was as dark as night.

The animals looked longingly for the sun.
Hopefully, they waited and waited. But not one
ray of light did they see. At last they cried out

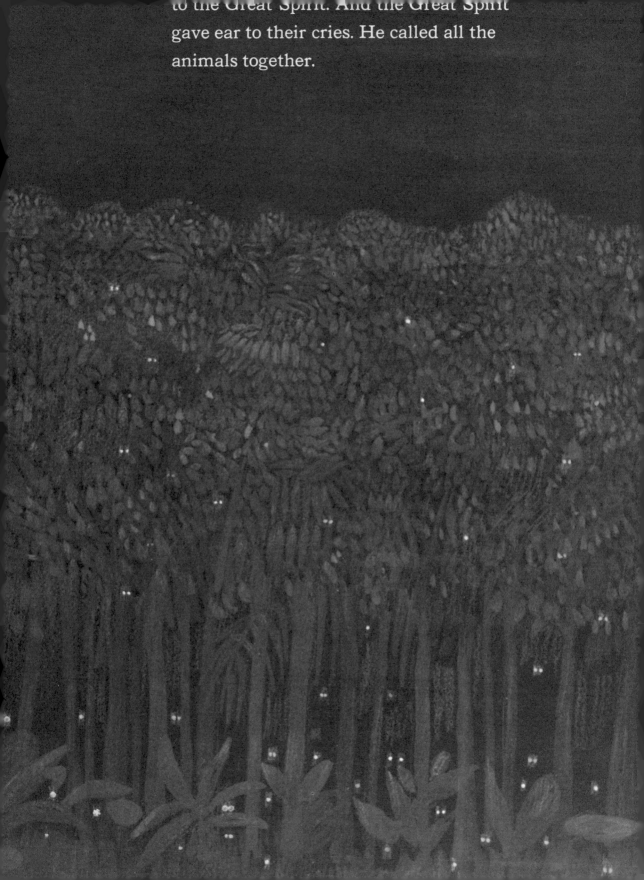

to the Great Spirit. And the Great Spirit
gave ear to their cries. He called all the
animals together.

"Tell me, oh bird," said the Great Spirit.
"Why did you not sing and wake the sun?"

"How can I ever sing again?" asked
the unhappy bird. "My heart is broken.
My six lovely eggs were cracked by those
five elephants."

"Pardon, Great Spirit," said the five elephants.
"We did not mean to do it. All five of us
were frightened by those four snakes."

"It was not our fault," said the four snakes.
"We were sleeping peacefully. Suddenly
those three squirrels landed right on top of us."

"But we couldn't help it," said the squirrels.
"The three of us were tumbled out of a tree
by those two boys."

"That was purely an accident," said the boys.
"The two of us were buzzed at and buzzed at
by that one pesky fly. He tried to make us fall."

"Let me see if I have this right,"
said the Great Spirit.

"The six eggs...
were broken by the five elephants...
who were frightened by the four snakes...
who were startled by the three squirrels...
who were tumbled down by the two boys...
who were buzzed at by one fly.

"So it seems to have begun with you, oh fly.
Tell me. Why did you buzz at the two boys?"

The fly did not know what to say. How could he
admit in front of everyone that he thought
he had knocked down a tree all by himself, alone?
So all he said was *Buzz, Buzz, Buzz.*

"Come, come," said the Great Spirit. "You can
speak as plainly as the others. Tell me
why you buzzed at the boys."

Buzz, Buzz, Buzz, said the fly.

"I shall give you just one more chance to explain,"
said the Great Spirit.

Buzz, Buzz, Buzz, said the fly.
And not one other word would he say.

"So be it," said the Great Spirit. "You would
not speak when I asked you to. So you shall
never speak again. From now on you shall
say nothing but *Buzz, Buzz, Buzz*."

Then the Great Spirit smiled kindly at the
mother bird. "When you return to your nest,
you will find your six eggs whole again," he said.
"Now, my child, sing and wake the sun."

"Oh, thank you," said the grateful bird.
She sang a beautiful wake-up call.
A rosy color appeared in the sky.
And the sun got up at last.

The mother bird returned to the hill.
She found her six eggs safely back in the nest.
So she happily cuddled them again.

The five elephants contentedly returned
to their own places in the field.

The four snakes went back to sleep in the grass.

The three squirrels chattered away on their very own branch.

The two boys went back to gathering nuts
in the tree.

And the fly returned to his buzzing in the
forest. Only this time he was careful to choose
a strong young tree upon which to rest.

Since that day the mother bird has faithfully
called the sun every morning. That is why
the sun has never been late again.

And since that day the silly fly has never
spoken another word.

All he can say is *Buzz, Buzz, Buzz.*